Puffin Books
Editor: Kaye Webb

Mulroy's Magic

'Magic?' said Nanny Mulroy, who lived in the flat
upstairs, 'You never know where you'll find it. All over
the place, magic is!' She certainly had come across more
magic than they ever did, the children thought enviously,
but of course she was ninety-five years old and things had
probably changed a lot since she was a little girl or a young
nursery-maid.

Take dragons, for instance. Nanny Mulroy had known a
delightful real dragon which she kept in the drawer with
her stockings until he grew and grew to the most enormous
size with all the good food she gave him, and was so useful
in getting rid of horrid bad-tempered Nurse Snapper. As
for witches, Nanny Mulroy had known at least two. There
was a beautiful, frightening, wicked one who enchanted
her with a magic potion when she was a little girl, and
pint-sized, capricious little Edie McBride, who took such a
fancy to the dolls' house that she turned a little girl who
played with it into a gasping goldfish. Yes, Nanny Mulroy
had seen things to make you open your eyes all right, and
lucky it was that she had been such a strong-minded,
resourceful person herself, quite able to keep her wits about
her when the magic turned awkward.

Six gay and funny stories to please almost everyone up
to nine, but especially perfect for family reading aloud.

Marjorie-Ann Watts

Mulroy's Magic

Illustrated by the author

Puffin Books
in association with Faber & Faber

Puffin Books, Penguin Books Ltd,
Harmondsworth, Middlesex, England
Penguin Books Inc., 7110 Ambassador Road,
Baltimore, Maryland 21207, U.S.A.
Penguin Books Australia Ltd, Ringwood, Victoria, Australia
Penguin Books Canada Ltd, 41 Steelcase Road West,
Markham, Ontario, Canada
Penguin Books (N.Z.) Ltd, 182–190 Wairau Road,
Auckland 10, New Zealand

First published by Faber & Faber 1971
Published in Puffin Books 1975
Copyright © Marjorie-Ann Watts, 1971

Made and printed in Great Britain by
Cox & Wyman Ltd, London, Reading and Fakenham
Set in Monotype Bembo

to Oliver and Stevie

Contents

1. Cross-doll

Once upon a time, there was a house by a river. It was large and tall, with a great many rooms: the River House, people called it. But that was long ago, and nowadays the house was divided into flats – it was too big for just one family.

Sometimes on rainy days, the children who lived in the garden flat would run upstairs to see a friend. Mrs Mulroy – Nanny Mulroy they called her – was ninety-five, and didn't get out of bed much these days, especially in winter.

'Tell us a story, Nanny, please,' they'd say. 'About when you were young . . . Please!'

'When I was young?' she'd say, folding her sewing, and laying it neatly in the basket. 'Such a long time ago! What can I tell you about . . . ?' Then she would begin.

When I was young, I lived here, as you know, to help with

a big family of children. Ten of them there were, and they had a nursery; and in the nursery there was a doll. He lived with the other toys in a dark green cupboard over by the window. The cupboard, which smelt of boot polish, was divided by three shelves. Most of the dolls sat on the top shelf. They all had proper names. But this doll sat on the bottom shelf with the bricks and the babies' toys. He had no name, you see; or not a real name. He was called Cross-doll, because he had such a cross face.

Poor Cross-doll. Nobody ever wanted to play with him. He either sat in the cupboard all day, or he got kicked around on the nursery floor, like a football. Once, the dog got hold of him, and that did not improve his appearance. His hair, which had once been red and curly, was now dirty and very thin. His clothes were torn, his shoes were lost, and his face! His poor cross face. One of his button eyes was loose, and his nose which was only embroidered on had come undone. All these things not only made him look cross, they made him feel cross as well. And the more cross he felt, the more cross he looked, if you see what I mean. The other toys got taken out and played with time and time again. But not Cross-doll. He sat at the bottom of the cupboard, looking more and more sorry for himself as time went on.

One day the children who lived in the house in those days, had a party. The nursery wasn't big enough to hold all their guests, so it was decided to use one of the big rooms downstairs.

Cross-doll listened to the other toys talking about it after the cupboard had been shut up for the night.

'They have cleared all the furniture out of the big ball-room and they are going to have it in there,' said a fat brown bear just above his head.

'I know all about it, I saw them polishing the floor when I went down with Jennifer this afternoon.' This was the Fairy Doll speaking. She was very new and pretty, having only been in the toy cupboard since Christmas. Cross-doll hated her. The Teddy Bear squinted down at Cross-doll through the slats of the shelf.

'I suppose they will take some of the better-quality toys down with them on the day,' he said, puffing out his chest. Naturally he meant himself by this.

'The newer ones you mean,' the Fairy Doll replied. 'What fun it will be. Do you think they will have games? ...' A green knitted Rabbit interrupted her.

'Last year they had a Punch and Judy show. Funny looking creatures they were. We saw them after it was over. They've got arms and heads but no legs!' All the dolls laughed. The Fairy Doll leaned over the edge of the shelf and looked at Cross-doll huddled up amongst the bricks.

'Almost as funny as having no nose,' she said in her high tinkly voice. The toys laughed again.

'You're a stuck-up Ninny,' Cross-doll shouted. 'I

wouldn't be you for all the gold in China!' But really he was very envious of the pretty Fairy Doll, as the toys well knew.

'I hear a Prince is coming this year,' the Rabbit said. 'Prince Rupert of Kleptomania.' (He meant Mesopotamia, of course.)

'Really!' The Fairy Doll opened her surprised blue eyes very wide. Then she added: 'I knew that already, Jennifer told me when – '

'You're a Stuck-up Ninny,' shouted Cross-doll again.

But nobody took the slightest notice of him. They chatted on about parties, the children they had known, and the places they had been to, until at last, one by one, they fell asleep.

All but Cross-doll, that is. He lay uncomfortably amongst the bricks, thinking how nasty and how unfair life was. He had never been anywhere. Not out of the nursery even. He had never had any fine clothes that took on and off; he had never been beautiful; he had never belonged to anyone, or not for very long. No one ever wanted to play with him, and worst of all, he didn't even have a proper name. He twisted and turned on the bricks, and frowned and sighed, and looked crosser than ever. But finally he, too, fell asleep.

The day of the party came at last. The nursery was tidied up, a big bunch of balloons hung from the ceiling. In the afternoon the children came to choose which toys they wanted to take downstairs with them for the party.

'I want Fairy Doll,' Jennifer said at once. She looked almost like a fairy herself, in her white frilly dress and silver slippers. 'Let's take the Rabbit and the Teddy Bears,' the little boys cried.

'I'll have the clockwork train and the box of soldiers,' the eldest boy said.

'Wan' my Humpy-dumpy-Man,' gabbled the baby.

And do you know, being such a large family, between them, they carried nearly all the toys downstairs.

Nearly. You know who was left behind. A pile of

13

bricks, an old engine with cracked wheels, and of course, Cross-doll. The engine didn't mind because he was too old to play boisterous games, and just wanted to be left in peace. The bricks didn't mind, because bricks are generally too stupid to mind anything. But Cross-doll minded a lot.

The children had left the door ajar, and from below floated up the sounds of the party beginning. The door-bell ringing, the front door opening and shutting, music, children laughing and talking, and running up and down the stairs. Cross-doll felt crosser than ever; he was missing it all. Then the nursery door was closed and he couldn't hear so well. But he knew that by now the children must be in the big ballroom, playing their games, dancing or per-haps watching another Punch and Judy show.

He had once been in the ballroom when he had first come to the house. He had been brought by Uncle Herbert on Christmas Eve, after the children were in bed. He remem-bered it as if it were yesterday. The huge room with its shining floor and glittering lights hanging from the ceiling; and the Christmas tree glistening and sparkling with silver and golden and coloured decorations. Uncle Herbert had wanted to put him on the tree there and then. But the children's mother had said: 'Oh, no, Herbert. He must be wrapped first.' But there were so many presents that year that there was no room on the tree for Cross-doll; and he had sat at the bottom instead, wrapped in crimson tissue-paper. He remembered Jennifer's face when she opened the parcel. All joy and smiles. He was the first big doll she had ever had.

Cross-doll always felt better when he remembered this part of his life, so he thought about it a lot. He was going over it again for the third time, when he heard the nursery door open, and somebody stole into the room quietly, oh! so quietly. Cross-doll listened and wondered who it was. You could hardly hear anything, but he knew someone was walking round the room on tiptoe, examining everything. Then, very slowly, the cupboard door opened, and a small pale face peeped in.

'Not one of our children,' Cross-doll thought. 'He's got red hair. Must be a visitor.' He frowned at the boy – for it was a boy – expecting him to shut the door again. But he didn't. He looked at Cross-doll and smiled. Cross-doll frowned even harder. He had forgotten how to do anything else, you see. The boy smiled again, put out a hand and touched his face.

'Come and talk to me,' he whispered, lifting him out. 'You look a nice quiet sort of person.' Cross-doll was very surprised. But there was more to come.

'It's too noisy downstairs,' the little boy continued, 'and I don't like crackers, or balloons that burst.'

Cross-doll didn't like these things either, so he stopped frowning and began to smile instead, just a little, at the very corners of his mouth.

'Let's play up here, shall we?' the little boy said, holding him on his knee. 'I tell you what, I will build you a castle all your own. You can sit by the window and watch. When it is finished you shall be King of it.'

So that's what they did. The boy built a high brick castle, with a special place at the top to sit in; and when it was finished, Cross-doll sat in it and was King. They played this game and other wonderful games for a long time. When it began to get dark, the boy turned on the light and told him stories. Cross-doll had never felt so happy.

'I like you,' the little boy said. 'I like your face; and you bend so well. What's your name?' But Cross-doll wouldn't tell him, because he thought that if he knew, the boy wouldn't stay with him.

It was long after six o'clock when the boy's mother came into the room.

'So this is where you are, Rupert.' She sounded surprised. 'All by yourself in here! Put the toys away now, we must go home.'

'I don't want to put this one away,' said Rupert, 'I like him.'

'Oh, yes. We must leave him ...' his mother was beginning, when Jennifer, who had followed her in, interrupted.

'Oh! We don't want old Cross-doll. You can take him – nobody plays with him any more here.'

'Well, if you are quite sure,' Rupert's mother said, and Rupert hugged Cross-doll.

So Cross-doll went home with Rupert, Prince Rupert that is. You can imagine what the other toys said when they heard about it.

'I can't think what he saw in Cross-doll,' the Teddy Bear said that night.

'He must be a very peculiar child, that Prince whatever he's called,' the Fairy Doll said with a sniff. 'Fancy wanting that poor broken old thing when he had all of us to choose from.'

But Cross-doll didn't mind any more what those dolls said about him. He was happy. His nose was sewn back again, and his eye mended. His hair was washed, and a little more added. He even had a new suit of clothes, although he didn't wear them much, as he felt more at home in the old ones. He was Prince Rupert's dearest friend. They were

never apart. They had their meals together, they slept in the same bed, they even did their lessons together. And when Prince Rupert grew up and became King, and Cross-doll was very old indeed, he sat on the great royal desk, between the inkwell and the large leather-bound diary, and watched what went on. All the people that came and went; all the meetings and the talks; all the Kings and Queens and the Important Men.

'What do you think of that, eh, Cross-doll?' the King would say sometimes, about nothing in particular, when he was signing letters. 'That's interesting, don't you think?' And Cross-doll would frown and smile, and think to himself: 'A lot more interesting than that old green cupboard. Yes, interesting, very interesting indeed.'

Or sometimes the King would say with a smile: 'We haven't thought of a name for you yet, have we?' And do you know they still haven't? Cross-doll is Cross-doll to this very day.

2. Edie McBride

'Tell us another story! Another one! Please! Please!' cried the children. Nanny Mulroy smiled and smoothed back the coverlet with her bony, wrinkled, old fingers.

'Just one more,' they said again. 'Then ... er ... then we'll fetch your tea.'

Mrs Mulroy leant back against her pillows. 'I don't know if I can remember any more. Pick up my wool for me, my dear. Now, let's see. Have I ever told you about the witch I met? Of course she was only a small one but she was a witch just the same, and clever, at that.'

One day I was sweeping up in the nursery after tea. Everything was very quiet. The children were downstairs with their mother, the gas-fire was singing and humming to itself, and I was feeling a bit sleepy, to tell you the truth;

the baby had kept me awake in the night; and then, as I stood for a moment looking down at the garden below, I heard a scritchety, scratchety, thumping, bumping noise coming from the toy cupboard. 'Lord save us,' I said to myself, 'there's mice in that cupboard.' I went to the door and opened it, all of a sudden. Whoosh! Like that. But there was nothing to be seen inside except the toys, which I had just put away myself. I closed the door and then opened it again slowly and quietly. Nothing happened for a while, and then before my eyes, a square tin on the top shelf, in which one of the boys kept his toy soldiers, moved slightly. It frightened me, I can tell you. Well, I stood watching it, and then I thought, there's a mouse *inside* it, of course; and I wasn't frightened any more. Mice don't scare me like they do some people. I took this tin over to the window and put it on the table. The lid was stiff and difficult to open, so I started looking in my work-basket for my scissors, thinking to prise it open. Then the box moved again and I heard a voice calling:

'Let me out! Let me out this instant, or I'll turn you into a – a – mushroom!'

I couldn't believe my ears. I thought it was one of the children playing a joke; and I looked all round the nursery expecting to see one of them hiding behind the screen, or the curtains. But there was nobody there except me. I looked at the tin. Somebody was thumping on the inside and shouting again:

'Let me out! Let me out, or I'll turn you into a snake, no – a fish!'

Well, I was only young, and I didn't like the idea of being a mushroom, a snake, a fish, or anything else for that matter. So I opened it, quickly, there and then.

Mrs Mulroy took off her spectacles and began to wipe them with a handkerchief.

'Yes?' whispered the children. 'Go on – who was it?'

It was the most comical little figure you ever saw. I had been frightened a moment before, but now I laughed. Edie McBride – I found out her name later – had a large head, and rather a small body in proportion. Her hair was straw-coloured and hung to her shoulders in terrible tangles. She wore a grey velvet dress, very much torn at the edges, red and black striped stockings, and a black coat, which had gone into holes at the elbows. I knew she was a witch because of her tall black hat, a bit squashed now, on account of being shut up in the tin. She was about four inches high.

'I don't know what you're laughing at,' said this little creature, staring at me fiercely; and I stopped laughing, because I could see that her feelings were hurt, and perhaps she had had a fright too.

'I am sorry I laughed,' I said, 'and I am sorry I shut you in the tin. It was a mistake. I didn't know you were there.'

'Hmm!' this little person said. 'You ought to be more careful!' She began to peer under the soldiers in the tin,

Edie McBride

and taking hold of one of them she tugged and pulled, trying to lift him. Of course he was much too heavy for her, being so tiny, so I lifted him for her.

'What do you want to do with him?' I asked, holding him up.

'Nothing! I'm looking for something,' she snapped. 'It must be here. I left it somewhere in this room last night.'

'What is it you've lost?' I said.

'My broomstick.'

'Oh, yes,' I replied, 'I remember seeing it. I thought it was one of the Dolls' House things, so I put it in there.'

'Fetch it then, you stupid girl.' She wasn't exactly polite, but I could see she was thoroughly upset at being in the tin. So I went over to the Dolls' House, and there, leaning against the wall in the kitchen where I'd put it that morning, was a tiny broomstick.

I gave it to her and immediately she hopped on, and started to buzz all over the room like some enormous insect. Round and round she went, until I began to feel quite dizzy, and sat down.

'Would you like a Dolly-sweetie?' I said at last, when I could stand it no longer. 'I've got some somewhere.' She swooped round once more and then landed on the table beside me.

'Where are they?' said she.

'Be a good girl then,' I said. 'Stay there and I'll fetch one.' She liked Dolly-sweeties all right. She sat on the edge of the table swinging her legs, holding the sweet with both hands, munching and crunching, and she would have finished the whole tin if I'd let her. She was much more friendly now, and told me her name, how old she was, and how she often came into the nursery in the evening, when no one was there, to play with the toys.

'But there's one thing I've never been able to play with,' she said. 'It's always shut; and if you don't let me play with it I'll turn you into a – a – a – frog.' She had finished the sweet by now, and stood glaring at me, swinging her broomstick.

'What is it you want to play with?' I said. I didn't really believe that a tiny creature like her could turn me into a frog. I was a big girl in those days.

'The Dolls' House,' came the answer.

'You can play in the Dolls' House in the evenings if you want,' I said. 'But mind you leave it tidy.' I wasn't going to be ordered around by her, you see.

'I'll leave it tidier than it's ever been!' she grinned at me, and danced a little jig on top of the tin. No sooner had I unfastened the latch, and swung the face of the house open, than she went flying in on her broomstick.

She loved that Dolls' House! Of course it was a particularly beautiful one. It had everything you can imagine. Real oak parquet flooring; carpets; Queen Anne furniture; electric lights that turned on and off; and a copper bath which you filled with a tiny jug. There were flowers in real glass vases in the drawing-room, and books in the shelves that actually took out. Some of them even had pictures printed in them. There were pillows and sheets and silk quilts on the beds; curtains at all the windows, even brass rods with rings to hang them from.

But I think it was the kitchen Edie liked best. I suppose they didn't have kitchens where she came from, poor little thing. It was a big room, and she ran round and round, examining everything. She opened the drawers and peered inside the cupboards. She counted the cups hanging on the dresser, and rattled the canisters on the shelves. There was water in the kettle and coal in the stove and an old black rocking-chair with a patchwork cushion to sit on. After she had looked at everything, she laid the table, first with a cloth, and then with all the crockery and cutlery she could find; and when that was done, she sat in the rocking-chair in front of the fire and began to rock herself.

I left her there with the window open, singing and looking at one of the tiny books she had brought down from the library upstairs.

After that, I often used to see her in the Dolls' House, and sometimes she would talk to me, and sometimes not. I would come into the nursery, quietly, in the evening – if you made a noise she was always gone – and there she'd be tinkering away with this or that. She seemed to enjoy moving all the things in the House from room to room. She was always at it. I looked in one evening and found all the cups had been moved from the dresser and were hanging in the bathroom instead. Or another time one of the beds had been moved down to the kitchen. I could see Edie fast asleep on top of the pink silk quilt with her boots on. The

grandfather clock had always stood in the hall; now it was in the dining-room. And the six dining-room chairs, with their red leather seats and carved backs, were now up against the schoolroom wall in a neat row.

The children who lived in the River House in those days hardly ever looked at their Dolls' House. They were so used to it, I suppose, or perhaps they just weren't interested. At any rate, for a long time Edie arranged the Dolls' House exactly as she wanted it and nobody noticed. Then one day another child came to stay, a cousin. She was the only one in her family, and used to getting her own way. Lucy, she was called. The first thing she said when she came into the nursery was:

'Oh! What a lovely Dolls' House! Can I play with it?'

I didn't quite know what to say. I thought of it as Edie's Dolls' House by now.

'It might be better if you played with something else first,' I said, thinking she'd forget all about it.

'No!' replied Lucy. 'I want to play with the Dolls' House now!' And play with it she did for hours.

'Somebody very silly has been in here,' she said to me several times. 'There's cups in the bathroom and a bed in the kitchen! And there's nothing to sit on in the dining-room.'

'Really?' I said, and my heart sank as I watched her changing it all. I didn't dare go into the nursery that evening. I knew exactly what Edie McBride would be doing.

In the morning there it all was, as she liked to have it. The bed in the kitchen, the dining-room chairs in the schoolroom and the grandfather clock up in the bathroom of all places!

'Look!' cried Lucy, pointing at the house. 'Somebody moved it back!'

'Never mind,' I said. 'Let's leave it, shall we, and do something else?'

'No!' said Lucy, and would you believe it she moved it back again. Of course it was easy for her, all she had to do was lift it up with her fingers. Whereas I had seen Edie staggering about with the grandfather clock, twice her size, and I knew how heavy everything was for her.

Well, this went on for several days. In the daytime the Dolls' House would be as Lucy wanted it, but as soon as the children had gone upstairs to bed, Edie would start to rearrange it.

'If ever I catch that child,' she said angrily to me one night, puffing upstairs with one of the chairs, 'I'll make her sorry she even so much as looked through the window of this house.'

'You are not to do anything to her,' I said, 'otherwise I won't let you play in there at all.' Edie muttered something under her breath, but I didn't take any notice. Perhaps I should have. All the same, I was looking forward to the day when Lucy was to return home.

Then one evening, I went into the nursery to fetch some ironing, and I found Lucy in her nightdress, hiding behind the toy cupboard, and watching the Dolls' House with big eyes.

'I want to see who it is changes it round, Nurse,' she said quickly, when she saw me.

'You foolish child.' I must have sounded cross, but really I was frightened. 'Go back to bed at once . . .' But it was too late. From the garden, through the open casement window, flew Edie, perched on her broomstick, her ragged black coat streaming out behind her. How she knew it was Lucy who had been rearranging the Dolls' House, I don't know, but when she caught sight of her she began to scream insults and abuse at the top of her tiny little voice. 'Now I've caught her,' she shrieked, swooping down in front of the astonished child. 'Wretched girl . . .' and she gabbled something in a language I couldn't understand, and waved her arms in the air. Then off she went again, out through the window, into the dusk beyond. I turned to look at Lucy. OH DEAR! What a terrible shock I had. She had gone! Vanished clean away. But on the floor, in a pool of water, lay a small goldfish, gasping for breath.

I had to think quickly. I picked up the goldfish and hurried to the hand basin. I knew perfectly well what had happened. Cousin Lucy was now swimming round and round in the wash-basin, opening and closing her mouth and looking very sorry for herself. What was I to do? What could I tell the children's mother? Lucy's mother? I watched the little fish for a time, and then to my relief, in flew Edie. She circled the room once, twice, a third time, and then alighted on the chimney of the Dolls' House.

'That's taught her a lesson,' she said, shaking with laughter. She began to open the skylight on the roof – that was the way she usually got into the house – but I shut it quickly, catching a bit of her skirt. She tugged and pulled, but she was caught fast.

'You have behaved very wickedly,' I said. 'It's not your Dolls' House; it is meant for the children. I said you could play with it in the evening, but not in the daytime.' I was angry with her, you see.

'You be quiet!' she shouted, as bold as anything. 'And let go of my frock, or I'll turn you into a – a – fish too.'

'Now listen to me,' I said. 'I agree it is very annoying to have all the things moved where you don't want them. But that doesn't mean you should turn Lucy into a fish. You behave well now, and turn her back again, and in the morning I'll bring you something much nicer than anything in the Dolls' House. But if you don't give Lucy back her proper shape, I'll take the Dolls' House down to the garden this very minute, and burn it, and everything in it.'

I said all this with my heart in my mouth, because I thought she might easily carry out her threat, and I would find myself swimming round the basin with Lucy. She stared at me with her head on one side.

'What will you bring me?' she said at last.

'Aha!' I replied. 'You'll find out in the morning.' The truth was I hadn't the faintest idea what I should bring her. I had only said this to try to change her mind.

'All right,' she said at last. 'But it had better be something good. Now let me into the House.' I undid the skylight catch and she climbed in. I heard her babbling to herself as she walked from room to room, and then there was Lucy beside me once more, crying and clutching at my apron, her nightdress a bit damp at the edges, but otherwise none the worse for her adventure. I comforted her as best as I could, and when I had put her to bed, walked slowly to my own room.

I sat and thought for a long time. What could I bring Edie? I thought and thought. She was a vain little creature; I had often seen her peeking and preening at herself in front of one of the mirrors in the Dolls' House. Something to make her look pretty perhaps? Suddenly I smiled, and got out my work-basket. I would make her some new clothes! She was pretty, you see, in a way, and yet she was always dressed in rags. Of course I wasn't certain if that was what she'd like but I thought I'd try.

And do you know, I sat up all night making her a complete wardrobe of beautiful clothes. I made her some drawers, and a white silk petticoat, trimmed with real Brussels lace, and remember she was only four inches high so it was a fiddly finnicky job. I made her a liberty bodice to hold up her stockings – they were always in wrinkles round her ankles. A red velvet gown, with a white piqué collar; and a black coat out of a piece of black silk left over from a dress of my mother's. When the first streaks of pink were showing in the sky, I was starting on the hat. It was black, too, and pointed, and in the front I put a tiny black patent leather buckle. I've never done anything so difficult.

At last it was finished and I had about ten minutes to spare before getting the children up. I went to the nursery and there she was, sitting on the chimney-pot waiting for me.

'You've been a long time,' was all she said. 'What have you brought?'

'Get down from there,' I replied, 'and then you'll see.' And when she was standing in front of me, I handed her five little packages, so small they almost slipped through my fingers. I had wrapped them in tissue-paper, and it took her a little while to get it off. I shall never forget her face when she saw those clothes.

'Oh!' she whispered, 'they're beautiful! BEAUTIFUL! Wait till the others see me in these.' I don't know who she meant by that, but she had her own clothes off in a trice, and was slipping into the ones I had made. She looked a picture in them.

'I must see,' she cried, and she ran into the house and up the stairs, to the long mirror which hung in the bedroom. She pranced up and down, and looked at herself this way and that. 'They are lovely!' she said again, appearing at the door. She stood for a moment smiling at me.

'Thank you for making them,' she said, 'and I am sorry that I was cross,' and with that she laughed again, jumped on her broomstick, and was off, round the room once or twice, and then out of the window into the bright morning.

I never saw her again. She couldn't bear the idea of sharing the Dolls' House, I suppose. Sometimes I wonder if it really happened. But she left these behind, you see, so I know she was real.

Mrs Mulroy pulled her work-basket towards her and lifted the lid. She rummaged about inside and then brought out a small cardboard box. She opened it and there, lying on a bed of white tissue-paper, neatly folded, were some clothes. A grey velvet dress, very much torn at the edges. A black coat with holes in the elbows, and a battered, pointed hat. All to fit a person four inches high.

3. Draco

'Of course, Edie McBride could only fly if she had her broomstick with her,' Nanny Mulroy said one day. 'But I did once know someone who could, well, fly properly!'

It was when I was in my first place, in a big house in London. Fifteen children there were in that family. Four sets of twins, all girls; then four boys; another set of twins; and right at the end, Alicia the baby. Their father and mother, the Duke and Duchess of Töst-Melba, spent most of their time travelling abroad. So the children had three people to look after them – (four actually, if you count the Governess, but she didn't stay very long): Nurse Snapper; Jones the Nursery-maid; and me, Under-Nursery-maid.

If the Duke and Duchess had known what a cruel, bad-tempered woman that Nurse Snapper was, I think they would have stayed at home more often. There was always one of the children standing in the corner; and very often several of them locked into the broom cupboard as well. The two eldest boys went to bed without their supper about three times a week. I felt dreadfully sorry for them all, and tried to help them as best I could. But that Nurse Snapper was a regular Demon – almost wicked, one might say.

Tall and thin, with small eyes, and a large red bony nose; she wore a long maroon-coloured serge dress, summer and winter, black creaking shoes, and steel-rimmed spectacles. Her hair was drawn into a tight little knob at the back of her head; and her white starched cap sat on the top as if it had been stuck there with glue. She was nasty to everyone. The children, me, poor fat Jones; just anybody she happened to meet. I was always catching it for not ironing this, or not washing that; having wrinkles in my stockings; not having my cap on straight. The children hated her, and I am afraid I did too. I liked my job; but not Nurse Snapper.

It was a very large grand house; almost like a palace, I used to think. The front windows looked out on a shady square; and at the back there was a huge rambling green garden, surrounded on all sides by hedges, trees, and high walls. You could get lost in that garden; and in the house, too, for that matter. Room after huge room on every floor. Passages, hallways, little landings, strange doors, which might have been for cupboards, or might have been for rooms. Even odd staircases winding away heaven knows where.

One day – it was my afternoon off – I was climbing the wooden staircase which led to my room, and I stopped for breath on the half landing below my attic floor. There was a door there, which I had often wondered about. Usually it was kept locked. Every day I went past, I tried the handle, just to see. Today it was unlocked; I opened the door and went in.

Inside was a huge, dusty lumber room. Feeble shafts of sunlight filtered through the shuttered windows, striking here and there, giving it a strangely striped mottled appearance. Trunks and boxes lay propped against large dusty bundles – of what? Blankets? Old clothes? Rugs? I don't know. There was a piano over by the window; and faded gilt chairs, neatly stacked. Several violins in cases hung on the walls. There were old toys; hoops; a stuffed bear in the corner; and in the centre of the room stood a massive table, covered entirely with an assortment of crockery, china ornaments, and different-sized candelabra. I was fascinated! I'd never seen anything like it. I sat down on an armchair behind the door, and looked at everything in the room. I must have been there, quite quietly, for a good few minutes. Then, suddenly, my heart seemed to miss a beat! One of the ornaments on the table moved – very slightly. It was a small, green, china Dragon – or so I had thought. I sat absolutely still, unable to believe my eyes.

'You're trying to trick me!' said a piping voice.

'I'm not trying to do anything,' I replied. 'Anyway, who is that speaking?' I still couldn't really believe it was the ornament. For a moment nothing happened. Then before my astonished eyes, the green china Dragon took a couple of steps across the table, turned its head, and looked at me.

'I am,' he said. 'I speak rather well, don't you think?'

'Er – yes!' I said. 'Where do you come ... I mean, do you – er, live here?' It was all I could think of to say. He hesitated.

'Well, not exactly,' he said. 'Although I have been here a long time. They think I'm an ornament.'

'You're not made of china then?' I said.

'I don't think so.' He spoke rather doubtfully, as if he wasn't sure.

'It must get very lonely in here,' I said. 'If you're here all the time?' The Dragon nodded his head.

'Yes. It does.' His voice sounded very sad and far away. 'But I don't know where to go. You see ...' he broke off, as footsteps sounded on the wooden stairs. I heard Nurse Snapper's familiar voice. '... Connie? Connie? Where is that dratted girl?' The Dragon looked at me mournfully.

'Good-bye!' he said.

'Would you like to come with me?' I whispered. He blinked once or twice, and nodded. So without thinking any more about it, I picked him up quickly and popped him in my apron pocket.

'Here I am, Nurse Snapper!' I called. She turned on the stairs.

'What are you doing in there, may I ask?' she said, frowning. 'You know very well, you are not supposed to go wandering all over the house! Anyway that door should be locked. Now, I need you this afternoon; that stupid Jones is ill, and there's all the ironing to do.' She sniffed. 'If I had my way, there wouldn't be any afternoons off! Girls like you – up to mischief . . .' She stared at me suspiciously. 'You're very pale, all of a sudden. I suppose you're sickening for something too!'

'No, no, Nurse. I'm quite well, thank you. May I please just go and get a – a handkerchief? Then I'll be straight down.'

'Well, hurry up; we haven't got all day.' She clattered off downstairs; I ran up to my room.

I could feel my new friend squirming about in my pocket, so I took him out carefully, and put him in my stocking drawer. I only had two pairs of stockings at that time, so I put in my winter woollen gloves as well, for him to lie on.

'Stay there,' I whispered. 'I'll be back presently. What do you like to eat?' He began to thrash his tail about – excitement I suppose.

'Er – dust!' he said eagerly. 'Flies? A bit of sand? But

porridge oats would probably make me grow better. I am on the small side, you know.' He looked at me anxiously. 'Nobody will come in here, will they? I am not very used to people.' I shook my head and closed the drawer, leaving a crack open for him to breathe.

What an age that ironing took. Two dozen pairs of liberty bodices. Two dozen best petticoats. Eight sailor suits. Seventy-five handkerchiefs, and all the baby's things. I thought I'd never finish. It was nine o'clock before I'd done. I told Cook I was going to feed the pigeons, and managed to bring a large bowl of porridge oats up to my room. I opened the door gently, so as not to give him a fright. There he was, curled up on my woollen gloves, fast asleep.

'Suppertime!' I said. 'Are you hungry?' He opened first one eye, then the other. As soon as he saw the bowl in my hand, he was out of the drawer in a flash.

'This – is – um – delicious – crunch, crunch ...' he mumbled through mouthfuls. 'But next time could you put some sand in it? For grit – strength!' he added. He flapped his wings and sidled to the edge of the chest of drawers.

'Can you fly?' I asked.

'Well – no. That's the trouble. I can't. I never learnt.'

'Never mind,' I said. 'I expect it takes time to learn.'

'You have to be much bigger than I am to be able to fly,' the Dragon said. 'I'll tell you what!' His face brightened. 'Can I stay here? If you could bring me some more oats, from time to time – there really wasn't much to eat in that lumber room – I shall grow much bigger. When I am much bigger, I shall be able to fly; fly away, fly right away – to – to – where I am supposed to be,' he finished rather uncertainly.

'Where's that?' I said. But he just looked at me with sad eyes and didn't answer.

'What's your name?' I asked finally.

'Dracothaurus is the species,' he replied. 'Er – I haven't a name of my own.'

'I'll call you Draco, then, for short,' I said. And that's how it began.

For a time we managed very well. I brought up quantities of porridge oats, and mixed it with sand I got from the children's sandpit; Draco lived very comfortably in my stocking drawer. Sometimes, when I was taking the children out for a walk in the park, I would smuggle him downstairs in a basket, or in my knitting-bag. Then he would frisk about in the long grass near the ornamental pond, smell the flowers, and turn somersaults along the path, just for the fun of being alive. We had some narrow escapes, though. Once a park-keeper saw him dashing through the flower-beds.

'Can't you read, Miss?' he said, pointing to the notice. 'It's wrote 'ere "All dogs must be kept on a lead". That animal there is out of control: if I catch you here again, I shall report you and your dog!'

Another afternoon, I was out with Alicia, the baby. I had taken the big twin pram, as there was more room in it. Alicia was lying asleep in one end, and the Dragon was sitting in the other. His legs weren't very long, and I had put him in because he kept lagging behind. We were

walking slowly along the tow-path, admiring the ships on the river, when who should I see coming towards me, but Mrs Timmins, who kept the little newspaper shop at the end of the road. She was only a few yards away. Fortunately she was very shortsighted.

'Out with the twins, are you, Connie?' She beamed at us; forgetting that the twins were much too big to sit in that pram now. She stopped beside us.

'My goodness! That young man doesn't look too good today, does he?' She pointed at the Dragon.

'No,' I said, hastily pulling the coverlet half over that very green face. 'He's got a cold; I'm just taking him home.'

Mrs Timmins looked worried. 'Take him straight home, dear; he doesn't look right to me.'

As I say, all went well for a while – until he began to grow. The more he ate, the more he grew; and the more he grew, the more he ate. The day came when he could no longer curl up in the stocking drawer. He must have been all of four feet long; very handsome, but definitely getting larger and larger.

'You're much bigger,' I said to him one day, stroking his green scaly back. 'Really very much bigger. Do you think you could fly yet?' He seemed quite excited by the idea. He crouched on the edge of the washstand and looked down at the floor.

'See if you can fly to the bed,' I suggested.

'One, two – three . . .! Here I go!' and he launched himself into the air. His wings beat violently, and for a few seconds he managed to hover quite well. Then, crash! He landed on the bed with a tremendous twanging of bed-springs.

'Ssh!' I said. 'Snipper-Snapper will be up here if you don't watch out. I must go now: I'll be back after tea.' And so it went on. I never felt lonely or homesick now, as I had at the beginning. The children seemed happier and the work not so hard. Nurse Snapper was just as disagreeable, but then nothing could change her. Or could it?

One day I came up to my room to fetch my knitting, expecting to find Dracothaurus under my bed, or behind the washstand. But no! He was nowhere to be seen. I searched all round the room: and then went to the open window. Had he been practising his flying and gone straight out into the garden? Below me, I could see the weather-vane swinging gently, and the orange tiles of the coach-house roof: and beyond, the garden, still and calm in the evening light. Then I saw him. There was a big pine tree that grew about fifty yards from the house, the tips of its spreading branches reaching far out across the garden. Dracothaurus was sitting on the topmost branch. I called to him:

'Draco! Draco! Come back. Someone will see you!' He looked at me and wobbled precariously.

'I can't! I'm stuck!' he wailed.

'Stay there! . . . Wait! . . . Wait for me . . . I'll think of something!' I turned, only to find Nurse Snapper standing behind me in the doorway, her bony nose redder than ever, her little eyes glittering.

'What do you think you're doing?' she said angrily. 'Shouting out of the window like a fishwife; and who at, may I ask?' She leaned on the sill and stared down at the coach-house roof. Fortunately, she couldn't see Draco. He had moved his position and was now screened by a branch.

'You try my patience to the limit, Connie! Now, go downstairs and get on with your work!'

There was nothing to be done. I just hoped that Draco wouldn't tumble off the tree, and hurt himself: and that no one would see him. Nurse Snapper kept me working until ten o'clock that night. However, when I eventually got back to my room, there he was, sprawled on my bed, looking very pleased with himself.

'I can really fly,' he said happily. 'I've done it several times; backwards and forwards!'

'Oh, you must be careful,' I said. 'Someone might see you.' I told him how Nurse Snapper had nearly seen him.

'She doesn't sound a very pleasant sort of person,' he said thoughtfully.

'She isn't,' I replied. 'I don't know what would happen if she actually saw you!'

'Do you think she'd be interested in this,' he said. 'Watch!' He opened his mouth, which was pink inside, not green, and a little puff of smoke came out.

'Goodness!' I said, half-horrified, half-delighted. 'However do you do it?'

Dracothaurus took a deep breath and blew out another larger cloud of smoke.

'I don't know. I felt I ought to be able to by now; and I just sort of huffed and puffed, and there it was. I wonder if I could do flames as well?'

He could, of course, and did; and soon a distinct smell, as

if of something burning, hung about my room. And what with the smoke, not to mention the flames, and Nurse Snapper, I was becoming very uneasy about the whole situation. But I hadn't the heart to throw him out, and so we went on as we were. He slept all day, and then in the

evening he would heave himself out of my tiny window, his great leathery wings flapping, his tail streaming out behind him, a few sparks left on the night air to show me the way he had gone.

How I hated Nurse Snapper! Jones the Nursery-maid had packed up and gone long ago, so now there was only me to do all the work. I washed and ironed, I cleaned and mended, dried tears, and wiped noses. But it was no good; she always managed to find fault somehow. It was all I could do to keep my temper.

One afternoon, I came into the nursery and found poor little Simon – he was only four – sitting all alone, with a plate of cold herring-roes on the table before him.

'What are you doing here?' I asked him. 'Why aren't you out in the garden with the others?' He looked at me with a woe-begone face. 'Herring-roes make me feel sick!' he said. Big tears rolled down his cheeks.

'I think you've sat here long enough.' I didn't like herring-roes myself. 'Now, stop crying; take that pinafore off, and run down to the garden. I'll take the plate.'

'And where will you take it?' Nurse Snapper's voice barked behind me.

'Perhaps you'd like to eat them yourself?' she added. I felt like throwing the plate in her face.

'He'd been there long enough,' I said. 'He's only four!' She stamped her foot. 'I'll not put up with this,' she shouted. 'Going behind my back, contradicting what I say . . .!' She was bright red in the face. 'You wait! As soon as her Grace is here' – the Duke and Duchess were in Italy and were due to return the following week – 'I shall speak to her; and then we'll see what's what, my girl!' She marched out of the room, her nose in the air, and slammed the door.

I took the plate of herring-roes up to Dracothaurus and told him what had happened.

'She'll get me the sack,' I said. 'I'm sure she will; as soon as her Grace is back. And then what will become of those poor children?' I felt sorry for them, left all alone with Nurse Snapper.

After tea, I went down into the garden with the youngest ones. It had been a hot day and we were sitting under the trees in the shade. Suddenly one of the older girls came running over to us, shouting.

'Connie! Connie!' she cried. 'Come quickly! Nurse Snapper is ill! She's fallen on the floor!' When I arrived in the schoolroom I found Nurse Snapper lying in a heap on the wooden floor, her starched cap knocked all awry.

'She's only fainted,' I said to the children, who were standing round in a circle watching. A strong smell of burning hung in the air. I opened the window and put the smelling salts under her nose. Gradually, she opened her eyes and sat up. She gave a little scream.

'I've been attacked!' she said. 'Attacked by a dreadful

Creature! A Monster – on the stairs; all green! Blowing flames and smoke!' One of the bigger boys winked at me, as if to say, 'She's gone barmy.'

'Flames and smoke?' I echoed, knowing very well whom she had seen. 'Surely not. You must have imagined it!' But she was feeling better; her temper was returning.

'Connie! Don't contradict me! I saw it, as large as life – a huge green thing – a sort of lizard, coming slowly down the stairs.'

'Yes, Nurse Snapper,' I said. A wonderful idea had suddenly sprung into my mind.

Dracothaurus was asleep on my bed when I came in.

'Have you been walking about in the house?' I asked.

'Er – the window is such a terribly tight fit.' He was very apologetic. 'I thought I would find another way out.'

'You met Nurse Snapper, did you?'

'Yes, there was someone there. She seemed – well, surprised to see me.'

'I think she was,' I laughed. 'Now, listen to me. I've got an idea, and I want you to help me.'

Nothing more happened for a day or two, then, when the older children were in the schoolroom, and the younger ones in the garden, and I was just starting the ironing, a terrible commotion began in the passage outside.

'Help! Murder! Fire! H-E-L-P!' The door burst open and

in rushed Nurse Snapper, screaming at the top of her voice, with Dracothaurus trundling along behind her.

'The Monster! The Monster! Don't just stand there, idiot! Do something. Throw some water over it! Help!...'

This was even better than I had hoped for. I said calmly, trying not to laugh:

'Monster? What Monster, Nurse?' For a moment there was silence.

'Can't – can't – you see it?' Nurse Snapper pointed with a trembling hand. 'There, look! – in the doorway.' I must admit Dracothaurus was a terrifying sight if you weren't used to him. He was enormous, a dark mottled green, with long claws on his feet, and a mouth gaping open, fairly crammed with teeth. He stood in the doorway, blowing smoke out of his nose, growling at us.

'There's nobody in here beside you and me, Nurse,' I said sweetly. I was beginning to enjoy myself. Nurse Snapper sank down on to the nursery chair.

'I think you've been overdoing it,' I said. 'You need a rest; you're seeing things.' She shut her eyes. I waved at Dracothaurus, who backed out of the room and waddled towards the stairs. I could hear his scaly tail rasping and scraping on the linoleum.

'Seeing things?' she whispered.

'Yes – I should go to bed,' I said kindly. 'I'll look after everything.'

You wouldn't think that someone like Nurse Snapper would crumple up so fast. But she didn't last very long after that. She saw the Monster once more – he put his head in at the window, and blew flames and smoke at her – then she left. She was overworked, she said, and her nerves were all to pieces. I don't think anyone was sorry to see her go. Except Dracothaurus perhaps.

When the Duke and Duchess returned I was put in charge of the children. I had someone to help me with the washing and ironing, of course, so I managed very well. I moved my things downstairs, and Dracothaurus continued to live up in the little attic room; and until the end of the summer we were all very happy. But, of course, I knew it couldn't last.

In September, when the nights were getting cooler, and the days were drawing in, Dracothaurus said it was time for him to go.

'Although we are so large, we are like the swallows,' he said one evening. 'We like a warm climate all the year round. So we have to fly South to find it.' I was sad; I had grown so fond of him. But he promised to return; and he did. Each year, in the summer-time, he came back to see me. He'd perch up in that great pine tree, balancing in the highest branches – it's a wonder nobody saw him – but people are terribly unobservant. Then when the children were all grown up, and I moved away, he still came; once a year, on my birthday, to wish me many happy returns and to bring me a present.

Nanny Mulroy took off her spectacles to polish them. 'It's my birthday today,' she said softly.

4. The Pirate Ship

'Did I ever tell you about the Pirate Ship?' Nanny Mulroy said one afternoon.

It was a warm day and she and the children were sitting on the grass watching the ships on the river. Nanny Mulroy sighed. 'Ships!' she said. 'When I was young I knew them all; big ones, small ones, smart ones, shabby ones . . .' She paused and took off her spectacles.

'What about the Pirate Ship?' the children said.

'Oh, yes! Well!' She put her spectacles on the end of her nose and looked at them over the rims.

'That was a queer tale; it really was. A very queer tale. I was only young at the time, but I've never forgotten it.'

My father was a miller, and we lived very close to the sea. We worked from morning till night in the mill, most days;

but one Sunday morning – it was hot like this – I was sitting idle on the jetty wall, making boats out of paper, and dropping them into the mill-race. For a while they floated there quite merrily; then some became water-logged and sank, and some were carried away to sea. The sea! The sea! How sad I felt: what wouldn't I have given to go to sea, or perhaps I was just tired of working so hard in the mill. At any rate, such a thing had never been heard of when I was young. A girl going to sea? I wouldn't even have mentioned it.

I was just making the last little boat when my father walked past.

'You be careful, my girl,' he said, looking at the little boat in my hands. 'Don't you sail 'em just before the moon is full, will you now?'

'Why not, Pa?' I said.

'They do say – "Sail a paper boat the day the Moon comes full, you'll find yourself in her before the dawn."' He laughed. 'Course it's only an old tale!' and he patted my head. Old tale or not, he clearly didn't believe it. I wasn't so sure. I stared at the little boats; they had almost disappeared. I could just see a few spinning away into the distance. 'I don't believe it either,' I thought, 'but there's no harm in trying. You never know!'

A week later, when a big harvest moon hung in the sky, I crept out of my little room, and down the stairs into the moon-lit garden. I was still in my Sunday dress; I was afraid that if I had put my night clothes on I would have fallen asleep. Across the grass, wet under my feet, and through the rickety gate which led towards the mill. That afternoon, the finest paper boat I'd ever made had gone spinning down the mill-race. I had given it three large sails, two small for luck, a rudder to steer with, and matchstick masts.

Everything was very still and quiet, except for the sound of the water slip-slapping in the moonlight, and the mill-wheel beyond me splashing and groaning, as it turned slowly round and round. My heart was thumping, I can tell you. Along the flagstone path, with the mill towering above me. Now I was on the jetty wall itself. I held my breath as I peeped over, hardly daring to believe my eyes – and then gasped. Rocking gently on the incoming tide, sails hoisted and fluttering, lay my ship! A three-masted schooner! I couldn't believe it! It couldn't be true! I stood for a moment or two taking in every detail. Then I noticed someone standing on the bridge.

'All present and correct, Captain,' sang out a voice. 'Chief Mate reporting.' A real live ship with real live sailors! Oh joy! I didn't wait a moment longer, but scrambled down the wall, Sunday dress, petticoats and all, and jumped on board. It was even better on deck. A really big ship; paint fresh and clean; fittings of polished brass; all smelling faintly of new wood and tarred rope. Above me the sails shimmered white in the moonlight.

The men were standing stiffly to attention; and I could see they expected some sort of order. I turned to the Chief Mate.

'Cast off, Mr Mate,' I said. 'We will make for the Southern Seas.' He gave the order, and immediately the sailors ran forward to loosen the mooring ropes. We were off; slipping smoothly through the water, with a light following breeze.

I shall never forget those first hours as we sped across the water. I stood on the bridge and watched the dark land move farther and farther away. Past the strings of coal barges moored in mid-stream; the dredger; the fishing boats; the little dinghies and smart sailing yachts; the lifeboats moored out in the bay. The tide was high by now, and on the turn, so we crossed the bar of sand which separates the sea from the river, without any difficulty. Above us the moon rode high in the velvet sky, and the water splashed and gurgled against the bows of the ship.

'Is this your first trip to the Southern Hemisphere, Captain sir?' said the Engineer, as we sat drinking our cocoa after supper. I didn't like to admit that I had never been on any trip anywhere. So finally I said:

'Do you know, I just can't remember whether I've been there or not!' The Chief Mate smiled. 'Oh, it's a fine climate down there and no mistake. I like that part of the world.'

'Too many pirates for me!' This was the Engineer.

They all laughed and shook their heads. I had always rather envied pirates and their bold bad ways.

'I'd like to meet some,' I said, yawning. 'But not now. Now I think it's time we got some sleep!' And so we prepared for bed.

For two days and two nights we journeyed on. We had a fair wind, and a calm sea. Then on the morning of the third day, when I awoke, the ship was at anchor. I put on my clothes and ran up on deck. What a sight met my eyes! The ship was moored in a little bay, almost surrounded by wooded hills. In the distance, mountains tipped with white rose up through the morning mist. The water was brilliantly blue, and so smooth and flat, it looked as if one could walk on it. I could hear parrots screeching and calling, and under the overhanging trees, scarlet flamingos stood, arching their long necks, and picking delicately amongst the shallows. Above it all, the sun cast its hot steaming rays.

'The Southern Seas, Captain,' said the Chief Mate by my side, 'and it's going to be a hot day. Will you be taking a morning dip, Captain sir?'

'Yes, I will,' I said at once. Swimming was another thing that girls were not supposed to do in my young days. But I could swim, because, living so near the water, it just came natural.

So after breakfast, I splashed and kicked and swam about to my heart's content. Good strong nets, specially made for the purpose, protected me from the sharks. When I came

out finally, the Chief Mate was waiting to speak to me.

'Captain sir,' he said, 'I propose to take the men in search of fresh vegetables and water. I know that there are abundant supplies on the mainland.'

'That's a very good idea,' I said. I didn't want to seem unfriendly, but I thought how nice it would be to have the ship to myself for a while. He gave the order; the men lowered the boats. Soon they were rowing quickly and strongly towards the mainland.

The sun shone down. The stays and timber decking creaked as the ship rocked gently. I was tired after my long swim, so I curled up in a hammock slung between the main hatch and the one remaining boat, and was soon fast asleep. When I awoke, it was to the sound of voices.

'Nothing 'ere, that I can see,' said one.

'The crew must be somewhere!' said another.

'Gone ashore for food and drink I dare say,' a third added.

Raising my head slightly, I could just see the speakers. Eight or nine men were clustered together before the fo'c'sle hatch. They were dressed in the strangest assortment of clothes you ever saw. One wore a red jacket and a striped skirt. Another, baggy pantaloons and a lady's frilled blouse. Some of them had their ears pierced with large gold ear-rings. They were all dirty and unshaven, and armed to the teeth.

'PIRATES,' I thought, a slight shiver running down my spine. I sat up in the hammock and leaned forward to get a better view. I must have leaned a bit too far, because the next thing I knew, I had pitched out of the hammock and landed sprawling on the deck beneath.

I scrambled to my feet. The Pirates were obviously as taken aback as I was.

'Wha–a–what are you doing on this ship?' I said quickly. I wasn't going to let them see that they had startled me.

'Blimey! It's a blooming kid,' muttered the man with a skirt.

'If you can't keep a civil tongue in your head, don't speak at all,' I said, trying to think of how my mother would answer if anyone were rude to her.

'Where's the Captain and the crew of this ship gone then?' said the skirted Pirate. He was evidently the leader.

'The crew – is – er – out, away – for the moment,' I replied, with my nose in the air. 'I am the Captain of this ship!'

'Oh, you are, are you?' said the leader. 'Well, we'll 'ave you then. Nice little hostage.' He drew out his sword. 'And it's no use struggling,' he added, taking a step towards me, looking very fierce. I didn't much like the look of him, I can tell you. But I wasn't going to let him see.

'Don't talk to me like that,' I said, glaring at him. 'And put that sword away, you might hurt someone; and then you'd be sorry!' The other Pirates looked embarrassed, and started whispering together. I suddenly felt very cross, being disturbed on my beautiful peaceful ship like that.

'And stop whispering,' I shouted. 'Either you take me or you don't. But hurry up and make up your minds!' That settled it. The skirted one picked me up under one arm, and in no time at all, they had bundled me over the side and into their dirty, evil-smelling boat.

Nanny Mulroy leaned back against her cushions.

'Yes?' cried the children. 'What happened? Weren't you frightened?'

'Well, I was, and I wasn't.' She shook her head. They were so very different from what I had imagined. They rowed so badly! 'You're all uneven,' I said. 'Look! Let me count, like this ... O-ne ... t-wo ... o-ne ... t-wo ...' (I'd been able to row since I was five – so I knew what I was talking about.) I told them they could improve a lot if they practised; and I could row so well because I had practised a lot. For some reason this made them very cross, and one of them said, 'That's the first time anyone's criticized my rowing!' So I told him what my mother always told me – 'It's never too late to improve oneself.' And I held the tiller firmly.

'I think I'll steer,' I said. 'It will make it easier for you. Now – one ... two ... one ... two ...'

The Pirate ship was moored in a small rocky cove, and except for the narrow entrance, cliffs rose steeply on all sides. Their ship was painted black and had scarlet sails. Somebody had painted 'Daisy' in white, on the stern, but there any attempt at making her presentable ended. The deck was littered with trunks and boxes. Heaps of golden coins, pieces of silver and unwashed crockery, were mixed with mounds of dirty clothes.

'Heavens! What a mess!' I said, as I was dumped down on the deck like an old bag of flour.

'Mess?' the leader said. 'Any more of you, young lady, and you'll walk the plank . . .' But he didn't say any more, as a small thin Pirate with a large drooping moustache came up to him, with a very dejected face.

'No dinner again,' he said sadly. 'Cook's lying down. Says he's got a headache.'

'Again?' chorused the others. They all looked so gloomy I had to laugh.

'And what are you laughing about? . . . You 'orrible little . . .' began the leader.

'Perhaps she can cook?' Drooping Moustache interrupted hopefully.

Oh, you should have seen the change that came over them as they crowded round me! I thought quickly. 'I'll – er – I'll cook your dinner for you,' I said. 'Er – that is if you promise to take me back to my ship straight after. No walking the plank or any of that?'

The leader looked at his feet. 'I was joking,' he said gruffly. What a lie, I thought, but I kept that remark to myself.

'What can you cook, Missie?' Drooping Moustache said.

'All sorts of things. Roast beef? Steak and kidney pudding? That would take too long. What have you got in the galley? Eggs? Cheese? Sausages?'

'We've got some sausages!' Drooping Moustache said eagerly.

'Right! I'll make toad-in-the-hole, green peas, Brussels sprouts and roast potatoes, and – er – trifle, with chocolate sauce.' The words came tumbling out; but actually I could cook quite well. My mother had seen to that. The Pirates looked at me with round eyes, all smiles, and in silence we walked towards the galley.

'I'm afraid I can't possibly cook anything in this,' I

said. The galley obviously hadn't been cleaned for years. 'And I'm not fetching the peas and sprouts, or peeling any potatoes; you'll have to do that yourselves.'

The Pirates must have been extremely hungry, because there were no complaints, and they set to with a will. In no time at all, the galley looked a different place. Drooping Moustache started peeling potatoes and two others went off to fetch the vegetables. I began work on the toad-in-the-hole. First I made the batter; then I chopped up the sausages. It was hard work, I can tell you, cooking for all those people. I had to use four large dishes for the toad, and I only just managed to fit them in the oven. They were sitting on the tray nicely browned, and I had finished the trifle, when there was a shout from the Pirate doing look-out duty.

'Ship ahoy!' he yelled.

The Pirates, who had been standing round silently, watching me cook, crowded to the rail, collecting their guns and their cutlasses as they went.

'It's the long boat from the young lady's ship,' one of them called out. In fact I had seen that already. My Chief Mate and my crew had come to rescue me.

I put the trifle on the tray, and picking it up with some difficulty – it was heavy, with all the food on it – balanced the whole thing on the deck-rail. Some of the Pirates were beginning to take aim. They had forgotten all about me.

'If you so much as touch a hair of their heads,' I shouted,

'I shall throw all this straight into the sea!' The Pirates turned round.

'It would be a pity,' I said, 'because it looks rather good.' It did. And it smelt good too. For a moment they hesitated. Then Drooping Moustache cried:

'No! No! Please! Don't throw it over! We'll hoist our white flag and they can come aboard!'

My crew were very surprised to see the white flag fluttering, without a single shot being fired; but they were even more surprised when they reached us. The Pirate leader must have been a bit ashamed at the state of his ship, because his men started tidying and dusting as if their lives depended on it. One man even began to wash down the deck. When my crew climbed aboard it was all pretty shipshape. I was helping Drooping Moustache to lay the table.

'Come to lunch, have you?' I said laughing. 'It's all ready.'

When the table was laid to my satisfaction, we all sat down and started our dinner. It was delicious, though I say it myself. The roast potatoes were crisp and golden; the toad-in-the-hole done to a turn. Even the vegetables were tasty; although instead of good garden peas, they were some outlandish thing they have down there. It was when we got to the trifle stage that the trouble began. In fact, if it hadn't been for that trifle, I suppose I might still be there.

I had doled out the trifle, and was adding chocolate

sauce, when one of the Pirates, a little fat one with a bald head, stood up.

'He's got more chocolate sauce than me,' he said, in a really nasty voice, pointing at the Chief Mate.

'Don't point,' I said, 'it's bad manners. Sit down and eat your pudding, or I'll take it away.' That settled that, and we started our trifle in silence.

I had flavoured the trifle with some rather dried-up-looking nuts I had found in the galley, and some peppermint creams I had happened to have in my pocket. Unfortunately I had forgotten, in the excitement of it all, that also in my pocket was a collection of mothballs picked up from the linen cupboard floor a few days before. Whether it was the nuts, or whether a few mothballs had got in by mistake, I don't know. But that trifle had a very peculiar taste. My crew were much too polite to say anything, but the pirates started to complain at once.

'She's trying to poison us!' one shouted, pointing at me.

'How dare you insult our Captain!' The Chief Mate jumped to his feet.

'You keep quiet – you – you ladies' man,' snarled the other, drawing his sword.

'Two can play at that game,' replied the Chief Mate, his face red with anger; and he too drew out his sword. Before you could say Jack Robinson, the two men were cutting and swiping at each other in a most alarming fashion.

'Oh, dear!' I thought. 'They'll all be at it in a minute.'

I was right; you know how men – and boys – love to fight! The scene that had been so peaceful and contented a few moments before, was suddenly transformed into a mob of shouting, cursing savages, brandishing their swords, and struggling and pushing this way and that all over the deck.

'It's all her fault,' shouted the little bald Pirate; and he began to hack his way towards me, where I was standing beside the half-open cabin door. I picked up a sword that had been knocked from somebody's hand and prepared to defend myself.

Nanny Mulroy stopped for a moment. 'I expect you find it hard to believe,' she said, smiling a little, 'but I was very nimble as a girl.'

'Yes! Yes! Go on!' the children said. 'What happened?'

'Well! There I was, with a heavy sword in one hand – my left hand, which was awkward; and the trifle bowl in the other. There was quite a lot of trifle left; enough for seconds all round, I should think. Things seemed to be getting pretty nasty. The Pirate confronting me gave a jab with his sword, so without thinking twice about it, I threw the trifle right out of the bowl, splosh, in his face. I spilt a bit on the way, it was so heavy, you see. And just exactly at that moment, a cock crowed. I don't know where it was, because I looked round to see if I could spot it in the rigging somewhere. Such a funny thing to hear on a ship. At any rate it made me think of the mill standing peacefully by the water.

'Oh! I wish I were home,' I cried suddenly. For a moment nothing happened; then gradually the din of men fighting and yelling, and the clash of swords faded, and I felt myself picked up and carried rushing and whirling through the air like a feather. After what seemed like a thousand hours all in a minute, there I was, standing in the

dim dawn light, at home on the jetty wall. There was no trace of the sword that I was holding so fiercely a moment before. I must have dropped it in my violent passage through the air. Far away at the farm on the hill, a cock crowed again. Once, twice, three times. The morning was coming: pale bands of yellow and pink were beginning to streak across the grey sky. I turned and crept into the house. I was so tired, I got into bed with all my clothes on.

There must be different kinds of time in different parts of the world. I had been away nearly three days and three nights, but no one had missed me. Where had those days come from? Where had they gone? At the mill they didn't even know I'd been up in the night. Of course I was scolded for ruining my Sunday dress; it was torn and crumpled, and had a lot of something that looked like trifle spilled down the front of it. Nobody could understand how I had done it.

'Anyone would think you'd travelled the length and breadth of this world,' my mother said, holding up my dress, before she washed it.

I looked at her puzzled face. She wouldn't have believed me: Captain of a three-masted schooner, sailing the Southern Seas?

'Yes,' I said. 'They would, wouldn't they!'

5. Mrs Figgis's Magic Mixture

Nanny Mulroy looked down at Tod, the tabby cat curled up on her lap.

'Cats are strange animals,' she said, watching him stir and twitch in his sleep.

'There's more to them than you think,' she added. 'Some of them.'

The light from the gas-fire flickered in patterns on the ceiling. Outside, the frost crackled on the window-pane.

The children looked up from their game of dominoes.

'Yes?' they said, expectantly.

'I think the most frightening adventure I ever had started with a cat.'

'Yes?' said the children again, coming to sit on the edge of her bed.

'I don't like to think about it even now.' Nanny Mulroy

picked up her knitting. 'Let me see? – how did it start? – I was wondering through the fields near my home one day – picking hazels, I think – when I came upon a small grey cat caught in a snare. He was exhausted with pulling and struggling, and he let me prise and work at the noose, without scratching me. The wire had bitten deep into the fur, leaving a nasty red wound. But finally I managed to free him.

'There you are, you poor thing,' I said at last, setting him down. 'That's better. Now, where do you live?'

Although I didn't exactly expect an answer, all animals and plants were my friends; and in my imagination at any rate we talked together often. So, when this little creature spoke to me, I wasn't at all surprised.

'You are very kind,' he said. 'Very kind indeed; if ever I can help you, in my turn – I will!' He looked as if he were about to go; so I said quickly, 'But I don't know your name, or where you live?'

'Timpkin, Tompkin, sitting in the Sunkin – that's what they say!' He looked at me with his head on one side, adding, 'I know where you live!' I didn't have time to say anything to this as, with that remark, he jumped up and sprang away across the field, limping on account of his foot.

About two years later, when I had almost forgotten him, I met him again.

As you know, I lived in a mill, right down on the edge of

the water. A little farther up the estuary, where it narrowed and became shallow, was a tiny muddy creek. And here, half-hidden by bushes, and overgrowing trees, with its own small beach and jetty, a cottage stood, surrounded by an overgrown orchard.

This cottage always puzzled me. It had been empty for years. But the roof was in good condition; there was glass in all the windows, and behind them lace curtains still hung primly. The door stood ajar, and although the orchard around was choked with weeds, the path up to the door was trodden down, as if someone went backwards and forwards regularly. Inside, the cottage was empty of furniture, but still dry and sweet-smelling, and in the autumn, apples and plums ripened and fell, and nobody was there to gather them. Nobody except me, that is. Because I often walked along that way, for curiosity's sake – and for the plums.

One day, on my way back from school, I came down to the cottage from the quarry-field above, and found someone there before me. A grey cat was picking and sniffing amongst the bits and pieces washed up on the little beach. He seemed to be searching for something: turning over the seaweed, slates and stones, again and again. I was sure it was the cat I had seen before. He had the same pale fur and yellow eyes. Also he limped; and looking closely, I saw that one of his front paws was missing.

'Timpkin?' I called softly, just to see. He had thought

he was alone, so of course he jumped. His startled pointed face looked up towards me.

'Oh! It's you,' he said, after a moment. 'You've grown. What's-your-name-er . . .?'

'Connie,' I said. 'What are you looking for down there?'

He didn't answer me at once, then he said, 'Something that's lost.' He turned another slate over, and then another, and sighed deeply. 'But it looks as if I'll never find it.'

'Perhaps I could help?' I suggested.

'No! No! You couldn't possibly. Quite impossible.' He sounded absolutely certain on that score; so, instead, I jumped down from the hedge and began to pick up the ripe plums that had fallen on the beach.

'You aren't looking for these, I suppose?' I said, after a while, pointing at a pile of stones just before me. I picked one up and held it out. It was a small smooth pebble, with a hole clean through the middle. Timpkin came and stood beside me.

'Those are mine,' he said briefly. 'They've all got holes through them.'

'Do you collect them then?' I asked him.

'If ever I notice one, while I'm searching for . . . for . . . Yes, I do!'

'What are you going to do with them?' I said.

'Keep them! You never know when they might come in

useful. They protect you ... against ... lots of things.' He stared at me through narrow yellow eyes.

'Stones with holes through the middle keep out the Evil Eye,' he continued. 'You always want to have one on you if you can.'

'Oh!' I said. I didn't know much about the Evil Eye. I sat down on the beach to examine the pile more carefully, and Timpkin sat beside me. They looked fairly ordinary stones to me, holes or not. There was a long silence, broken only by the sound of water, and the gulls squabbling and screaming on the mud-flats beyond us. I forgot about the stones, and began to think about the place itself.

'It's very peaceful here, isn't it?' I said finally.

'Yes; it is – now,' came the reply.

'Who do you think lived here?' I was wondering what he meant by that 'now'.

'Somebody who's much better not here.'

'Did you know whoever it was – then?' I looked down at him, but could only see the back of his head. Silence.

'Who lived here, Timpkin?' I asked again.

'A bad, bad woman,' he muttered, as if to himself. 'Bad all through she was. As bad as they are made,' he added, more loudly as if he hadn't made it clear enough.

'What happened to her?' I looked down at him and saw that all the fur on his back was standing straight up, like bristles on a hairbrush.

'She's gone – away; for the moment,' he said slowly.

'But I have a feeling she may come back. I'm not sure.'

I didn't really understand this conversation; and Timpkin didn't seem inclined to continue with it, so we sat there quietly, looking at the water, until it was time for me to go home.

After that, I often saw him there: always in that particular place. Never anywhere else; and always searching for whatever it was he was looking for. Although he would never tell me what it actually was. Of course, I became curious, and sometimes I too, when I thought about it, turned over stones and seaweed, looked under the roots in the hedge, and in the crevices of the jetty, wondering what it was I was looking for.

It was a hot summer that year. August had come and gone; the harvest was in, and now September was here again, with blackberries in the hedges, and our apple trees heavy with fruit. One evening a storm blew up: and all night I could hear the buffeting of the wind, and the scratchy pattering of the rain on my window. By the morning, it had blown itself out, and all was still and calm once more. After breakfast, it being a Saturday, I was sent to do the shopping. I'd finished all my errands, and was on the way home, when I decided to make my way back along the shore to see if anything interesting had been blown in by the storm. It was a very wet and muddy walk. There were the usual boxes and tins, and pieces of wood; a great deal of seaweed, and some quite large branches. But it wasn't until I came to the little creek with the orchard that I saw something which made me stop. Bobbing about on the water, half-submerged, was a small bottle. Nothing unusual in that; but it was the colour that caught my attention. It was a brilliant purple; fairly dazzling in the sunshine. I

waded into the water and soon had it in my hands. The glass really was a beautiful colour: and the bottle itself a very unusual shape. I took the stopper out, and sniffed. How can I describe that smell? A sweet clear enticing scent: a mixture of oranges, toffee bubbling, apples stored in the winter, jasmine, fresh nuts in warm sunshine? A wonderful intoxicating smell. I looked at the label. It was stained, and a bit torn, but I could make out some of the words. 'Mrs Figgis's Magic Mixture' I read '... makes you more beautiful than you've ever dreamed. Drink this and ...' part of the label was missing here, so I couldn't make out any more. Above the words was a picture of a woman –

Mrs Figgis, I suppose. She didn't look *so* beautiful; she had a nice nose, and her hair was long and curling, but her eyes were a bit too close together, and had a strange look in them. I sniffed again, and again; and then tasted the liquid. The taste was even better than the smell. I took a few sips. The bottle was only half full. Perhaps it would make me more beautiful? I took a few more sips, and a few more, and then swallowed the last drops in one gulp. The moment I'd done it, I wished I hadn't. After all, I didn't really know what was in it. Never mind, it was done; and without thinking too much about it, I rinsed out the bottle, and put it in my pocket.

And swinging my shopping basket, and whistling gaily, I continued on my way home. Half-way down the lane I met Mr James the Postman.

'Hullo, Mr James,' I cried. 'Look how beautiful I am!' He didn't answer; he didn't even look at me! Old pig, I thought. But he was very deaf, so I put it down to that. Outside the mill gate Winnie and Doreen Smithson were sitting in the long grass, making daisy chains.

'Have you come to play? I called from the road. No reply. They went on talking to each other, as if I had said nothing. How unfriendly people are today, I thought, and ran into the yard and through the open kitchen door. My mother was standing ironing.

'Phew! I'm hot,' I said, meaning I'd like a nice cool drink. My mother didn't even look up.

'Ma!' I said. She put the iron down on the stove and walked over to the window. 'Connie's late.' She spoke as if to herself. I thought she was teasing me about being late home with the shopping.

'MA!' I was laughing. 'Look! I'm here! Stop pretending.'

But she wasn't pretending. I just wasn't there – for her; or at any rate, she couldn't see me, or hear me. I remembered Mr James, and Winnie and Doreen. They hadn't seen me either. And then the most awful thing of all happened. There was the sound of running feet outside in the brick yard, and a little girl carrying a shopping basket came in. She was about my age and dressed – yes! – dressed exactly like me. She even had the same patterned dress, and the same coloured hair ribbon. A horrible suspicion came into my mind. I looked at her socks. I had put on odd socks that morning, as I hadn't been able to find a pair. The little girl was wearing one grey sock, and one blue one. I felt quite sick with horror. *I* had vanished, and somehow, in some awful way, there was someone else walking about, pretending to be me.

Connie number two was talking happily to my mother; and my mother, all unsuspecting, was taking the shopping from her and laughing and smiling. Now she was pouring out milk for her to drink. I suddenly felt terribly angry; and tried to push the pretend Connie away. But I couldn't get at her; it was like pushing water. She knew I was there

77

all right. She turned her head, and looked at me, and smiled, a horrible sly little smile. And as if in my own head I heard her whisper:

'You can't get back. It's just too bad. I'm here now. Go away!'

Go away? Where could I go to? There was nowhere. I stood out in the lane miserably, wondering what to do. The sun still shone; the birds were singing. It seemed impossible,

but it had happened: and what was I going to do? I started to walk, hardly knowing which way I was going. I ran along the mill wall, and then down across the quarry-field towards the hidden creek and its little cottage.

Once there, I sat on the beach and thought about what had happened. It was the bottle, of course – or what had been in it. Mrs Figgis's magic mixture. It was magic all right; I knew that now – too late!

I must have sat for some time when a slight sound behind me made me turn. The cottage stood as it always had, surrounded by its orchard; the door slightly open, the curtains at the window stirring in the faint wind blowing from the water. It was the same, and yet there was a difference. I got to my feet, and walked up the path, noticing with surprise that the grass beneath the apple trees was short; somebody must have cut it. I pushed the door open and stood on the threshold looking in.

For a moment I thought I was seeing things. The room was full of furniture! I rubbed my eyes, but it didn't disappear. A heavy table, laid for tea, stood in the centre of the room, with wooden chairs grouped around it. A tall grandfather clock clicked and wheezed in the corner; and a dresser stood against the wall, covered with gleaming china. I realized, staring at the table, how terribly hungry I was. Someone had taken a lot of trouble to make a delicious meal. Chocolate cake, ham sandwiches, flap-jacks, fruit, little jellies. My mouth watered.

What made me hesitate? Until this day, I don't know what it was, but something about that room frightened me; and I knew as plainly as if someone had spoken aloud, that the more I took from this strange place that was gradually unfolding before me, the less chance I had of ever finding my own dear familiar world again. 'It's the same as the bottle!' I thought suddenly. 'I mustn't – I mustn't go in!' I stepped back and, slamming the door behind me, ran down the path as fast as I could. Once on the little jetty at the end, I stood uncertainly wondering what to do next. Then – oh what a relief! – I saw Timpkin picking his way across the muddy shale.

'Timpkin!' I called. 'TIMPKIN! Please help me, quickly!' Was I invisible for him, too? No, he came hobbling towards me, and a moment later I was telling him all that had happened. He looked rapidly towards the cottage. The door was still closed, although I thought I saw a movement at one of the upper windows.

'Don't on any account go in there!' Timpkin said; then, 'Have you still got the bottle?' I felt in my pocket. Yes, there it was: still with that faint enticing smell.

'Good! Now, do as I say. We must hurry! First the stones. She doesn't know we have those. You must arrange them in two circles, so that we can sit inside. You do it – it's so difficult for me with one foot gone.' I found the two heaps of stones, and laid them edge to edge, side by side, in two neat circles. Together we stepped inside them.

'I knew she was trying to get back,' Timpkin said, 'but I didn't know how to stop her, with that lost.' He pointed at the bottle in my hand.

'Who?' I said. 'Who's trying to get back?'

'Oh – lots of them,' he replied vaguely, 'but I think . . .' He broke off, and at that moment we heard the door of the cottage open, and someone came out and, screened by the orchard, began to walk down the path towards us. I turned to Timpkin.

'What are we going to do?' I whispered. I was frightened.

'We are safe enough, as long as we stay inside these circles,' he said. 'We must just wait for the tide to come up.'

At that moment, footsteps crunched behind us on the beach and, looking up, I saw a tall heavily built woman standing staring at us. She was dressed in a long loose-flowing gown, and her thick curling hair fell to her waist. She was handsome, beautiful even; only her eyes gave her away. Hard and cruel and set too close together, they glittered and flashed in her long brown face. I knew her at once. It was the woman whose picture I had seen on the bottle.

'Mrs Figgis?' I breathed to Timpkin.

'Yes. She can't do anything, or say anything; as long as we stay inside these stones,' he whispered. 'We must just wait for the tide. Then we'll fill the bottle – as it was this morning – that's the important thing. You drink it, and—'

'Ordinary salt water?' I interrupted.

'It isn't what's inside the bottle, it's the bottle itself that counts . . .' He was talking more to himself than to me. 'She left it hidden, of course. The storm must have dislodged it – I knew she'd try to get back; I've known it all along.' Timpkin shifted his position and glared angrily at the figure in front of us.

I felt very muddled. There were such a lot of things I didn't understand. Who was Mrs Figgis? Was it her cottage? Were Mrs Figgis and the little girl the same person? And how did Timpkin fit into it all? But somehow, with those angry, glittering eyes watching my every move, like a cat watching a goldfish in a bowl, the question died on my lips. And so we waited; and Mrs Figgis waited too, prowling slowly round us, as if seeking a way into our invisible fortress.

It was evening by the time the tide had started back towards us across the mud. We let the water actually trickle over the stones which surrounded us before we filled the bottle. I found myself repeating some queer rhyme – I can't remember it now – and then quickly I drank the rather salty water we had just scooped up. I don't know what I expected then. A thunderclap perhaps? A flash of lightning? But nothing like that happened at all;

the tide just came on in, spreading imperceptibly around us. I was very wet and cold. But Mrs Figgis had vanished.

'Has it worked?' I said at last, anxiously.

'I think so. You'll have to go back to the mill to be sure.'

Timpkin looked at me with his head on one side. 'Go on,' he said, 'you'll be all right now!' I said good-bye and ran towards the mill.

The moment I walked into the kitchen I knew it had worked. My mother was sitting at the table peeling apples. She jumped to her feet the moment she saw me.

'Connie! Where have you been?' She sounded very cross. 'Running out and disappearing like that, in the middle of a sentence. You frightened me to death. Your father's out looking for you now. You've been gone such a long time, we thought you'd fallen in the water.'

I could see she was angry because she was frightened. I had been terribly frightened too; so I put my arms round her and kissed her.

'I'm sorry,' I said. 'I'll never do it again. Never!' And I hugged her until I was forgiven.

About a month later, I went with my father to look for cockles amongst the mud-flats. To reach the spot he'd chosen, we had to cross the little beach below the cottage. When we got there I had a shock. The orchard and the jetty were still much as they had been; but the cottage had vanished, almost completely. Only a few mounds and uneven heaps of stone lay crumbling amongst the nettles, to show where it had stood.

'Where's the cottage gone?' I said aloud, very much surprised.

'Cottage?' echoed my father. 'There's been no cottage here for years that I know of, lass. There was a ruined cottage here when my father was a boy; the Witch's Cottage, they called it. But that fell down – Oh! – long before you were born.'

The Witch's Cottage! I was beginning to understand at last! What about Timpkin? Once he'd got the bottle, he'd found what he was looking for, I suppose. Was he a witch, too? Perhaps a witch's cat. Anyway, I never saw him again. But I've always looked at cats with a special eye since then; and I've always collected stones with a hole through them. After all, you never know when they might come in useful, do you?

6. The Magic Poppy

'Magic? You never know where you'll find it. All over the place magic is. Everywhere!'

Nanny Mulroy picked up her knitting, pulled the rug over her knees, and settled herself comfortably in the big arm-chair before the fire.

'I'll tell you something that happened to me, when I was quite young – not more than six or seven, I should think.'

One day, very early in the morning, I decided to get my father some bait. It was his birthday on the Sunday and he was a keen fisherman. I put on my oldest clothes, and tip-toed downstairs to fetch the bait-pot, and a fork from the kitchen. I didn't want anyone to hear me – it was to be a surprise.

It was a beautiful summer morning, cool and fresh, with dew shining on the grass and a salty drying-mud smell coming in from the estuary. As I skipped along the lane, admiring the flowers, and kicking up a dust with my feet, I sang this song:

> *Giants are red, Giants are blue,*
> *I'd like to meet one, and so would you.*
> *Under the earth, over the sea.*
> *Up in the clouds, that's where I'll be.*

I'd found these queer lines in a book of my father's, entitled *Magical Rhymes*. There were lots more, but this was the one I liked best. So I sang it whenever I remembered, hoping that something magic and exciting would happen, which it did, as you shall hear.

I had got my bait – several fat lugworms wriggling in the jar – and was on the way home, when I noticed an extra large poppy growing all by itself at the side of the lane. I think I knew at once there was something strange about that poppy. It was so tall, nearly as tall as I was. The flower itself was huge, and glowed red against the green grass, like embers glowing in the dark. I'd never seen such a beautiful poppy. My mother would like to see it, I thought, I'll take it home to show her. And I bent and picked it. I stood for a moment admiring the glossy petals and slender stem. It was as if all the poppies I'd ever seen or thought about were contained in this one flower. I must have stood there dreaming for some little time, and I jumped when a sudden rumble of thunder sounded, not very far away. Two crows, who had been picking over the stubble in the field behind me, flapped heavily into the air: and as they flew over me, I could have sworn I distinctly heard one of them croak, 'Look out! Look out! Giants about! Giants about!'

Giants about? I thought, quite forgetting the song I had been singing earlier. I don't think I want to meet any giants just now; I'd better hide – and I climbed up into the hedge, which was very thick and deep at that point, and waited.

It was very quiet suddenly; too quiet! The birds had stopped singing, I noticed, and the sky had become black and threatening. CRASH! – thunder pealed again, right over my head, it seemed. The trees and bushes which lined the lane began to stir and bend, and a cold wind rushed past me.

There is something coming, I thought, my heart missing a beat. Is it a giant? And as I crouched in the hedge hoping I could not be seen, I thought of the words of the song.

The ground beneath me began to tremble and shake. I had to hold on to the branches around me to keep my balance. Then, through the tangle of leaves, I saw a blur of blue and red, and an enormous pair of legs striding towards me, up the lane. One, two – one, two! Oh, those great legs! Giant legs! Nearer and nearer they came. Then,

instead of swinging steadily past me, and away, they began
to slow down, until finally – Oh, horrors! – they came to
a halt right beside me. He'd seen me! I was sure of it. Far
above, a great voice shouted. I couldn't understand what
he was saying at first, but gradually I made out the words.

'WHERE'S THE MAGIC POPPY GONE?' The ground

fairly shook. 'THE POPPY, WHO'S TAKEN IT?' roared the giant again.

I suppose he can see the broken stalk, I thought, flattening myself in the hedge, and putting my hands over my ears. At any moment I expected to be snatched up and crushed to bits. But after bellowing and stamping, and poking about in the hedge, he moved off down the lane, cursing and shouting threats.

Phew! I thought, feeling rather hot and uncomfortable. That was a near thing! I looked more carefully at the poppy I held in my hand.

'I'm sorry I picked you – if you're magic.' I said. 'But I didn't know. Are you magic?' I added, staring into that shining black eye at the centre.

It's difficult now, after all this long time, to describe the thin whispering voice that answered me. Very far away, yet very close; like leaves rustling or a thought in one's own head.

'Magic?' came the reply. 'Yes – yes – oh yes – magic . . .' I had to listen carefully to catch the words.

'Who else knows about you? Where do you come from? I mean I've never seen you before!' I said, all in a rush.

'Farrenfeugh,' the whisper continued. 'I am a Farren-feugh Poppy. There used to be lots of us, but now that the wicked Slintingriel has seized the throne, you know, I think I am the only Poppy left . . .'

'The Giant I just saw?' I interrupted. 'How awful.' I

didn't like to ask what had happened to the others. Twisting his beautiful red head up towards me, the Poppy continued:

'He keeps his poor sister, the Queen Bodina, and all her court confined in her palace, at the top of a high tower. And he has carried off the King, her husband ... taken him ... yes ...' the faint voice trailed away, and I sat considering this sad story. The Poppy's head was drooping, and I could see he was beginning to wilt. I felt sorry for the poor King and Queen of Farrenfeugh, but it was more to cheer him up than anything that I said:

'Perhaps I could help?' There was a pause. The voice that answered me sounded a little stronger, a little more hopeful.

'Could you? Perhaps you could?' He seemed to be considering the idea.

'You would have to come with me now,' he said; then, surprisingly, 'Do you suffer from heights?' I shook my head.

'There's no time to lose, if you are coming. I'll just increase my size a little; I don't think I could lift you at all at the moment.'

Lift me? What did he mean? I soon found out. I have told you that the Poppy was large, but I wasn't at all prepared for what happened next. He began to grow taller and taller in front of my very eyes, shooting up before me, twisting and turning on his green stalk. He must have been at least eight feet high by the time he stopped.

'Amazing!' I said at last, feeling quite dizzy.

'I can get bigger than this,' the Poppy said, his voice deep and booming now. 'But I think this will do. Hold on! It's not difficult – we float away – like this!' I held on, as I was told, and was borne up and up, into the tranquil morning sky. I wasn't exactly pulled along; rather we floated together, the Poppy guiding me. Butterflies flitted past us, and occasionally swallows darting after them. Faint noises came up from the country beneath us; my legs trailed out behind me, and we floated higher and higher.

There was a faint haze over the land below, so it was difficult to pick out any landmarks. We drifted on and on, the Poppy waving his petals like a jelly-fish in the sea. Stars began to appear, cold and wet-looking, although it was daytime. I tried to touch one or two, but somehow I never could; even though they seemed near enough. Just as I was beginning to feel rather sleepy, the Poppy said, 'Here we are,' and looking down I saw some roofs and turrets, and a high stone tower sticking up out of the trees. In the corner of the tower was a heavy wooden door.

'Can you knock? – twice, please,' the Poppy asked, in his muffled booming voice, as we hovered for a moment beside it. I leaned forward and knocked. There was a rattle of bolts on the inside, the door opened, and we floated through into the dim cool room beyond.

When I became accustomed to the poor light, I saw that the room was crowded with people; and what very strange people they were. All sizes and shapes, thicknesses and heights. One figure, standing in deep shadow in the corner, looked more like a very large grasshopper than a man. Over by the window, which was shuttered on the inside, stood two extremely tall soldiers. They were quite a bright green all over, and so thin and spindly they could easily have been mistaken for sticks. Then there were other figures, almost as strange: courtiers, soldiers, and some small rather fat little people, dressed entirely in grey leather. In fact, looking closely at them, I'm not sure their faces weren't of leather too. Standing in the centre of the room was a young woman, with a pale face and long greenish-coloured hair. Her dress was light green too, and covered with pearls and precious stones. On her head was a silver crown.

'Your Majesty!' the Poppy said, bending his stalk in the middle, and practically touching the floor with his heavy head of petals. 'Your Majesty, I have brought you a visitor!'

'Good morning, ma'am,' I said politely, although I couldn't help staring at her long green hair. The Queen, for of course it was she, came over to me, and took me by the hand.

'What is your name?' she said softly. I told her, and where I lived, and how by chance I had seen the Giant Slintingriel, or anyway his legs.

'My wicked stepbrother,' she said sadly, 'the two-headed Giant Slintingriel: wicked and cruel. He forces me and my

court – those that are left – to stay in this tower day after day. He has stolen the Magic Looking-Glass and the Silver Pipe. He has carried off my husband the King to the Giant's Castle beneath the mountains; and now he roams the beautiful country of Farrenfeugh, pillaging and destroying wherever he goes.' She covered her face with her hands and began to weep bitterly.

The courtiers crowded round her and tried to comfort her. I felt very sorry for her, and wondered how such a beautiful creature could have a two-headed giant for a brother.

'I'd like to help you,' I said, 'if I can. But . . .'

'We must somehow find the King,' the grasshopper person interrupted from the corner. 'Once our King is sitting on his throne again, Slintingriel will lose his power. But to find the King we must have the Silver Pipe,' he added.

'He took it from me again this morning,' sighed the Queen, drying her eyes.

The Poppy, who had been listening to this conversation, with his head bent forward, straightened himself, and began to twirl round on his stalk. Then he called out in a surprisingly loud voice, 'Silver Pipe – Silver Pipe – hear me now, and tell us where you are!' Someone opened the shutters and everyone turned his head expectantly towards the window. We stood waiting silently: I wondered what was going to happen. Below us the trees whispered amongst themselves, swaying a little in the summer breeze. Suddenly, silvery piping, very high and sweet, falling like angels' music upon the ear, swelled out from somewhere deep in the forest.

'There it is!' the Poppy cried. 'He's hidden it somewhere in the forest. Come, child! We must find it quickly.'

'And where will you go then?' The Queen clasped her hands together anxiously.

'To find the King, beneath the mountains. Who else can go, Your Majesty?' The Poppy's voice sounded strong and sure, and I began to tremble with anticipation and excitement.

'Climb up, child, and fold my petals over you for warmth; it is cold where we are going.' I did as the Poppy asked; we said good-bye to the Queen and her court and floated out through the open window.

The tinkling fragile music showed us the way to follow, and we soon found the Silver Pipe playing sweetly to itself in a tangle of briar. The bush was very prickly, and the Pipe difficult to reach, but in the end I had it in my hand, and we soared away high above the trees.

'If we had the Magic Looking-Glass as well . . .' the Poppy said. But he left the sentence unfinished, as if that were more difficult.

'But why does he hide them?' I asked. 'Why doesn't he take them with him?'

'They are only magic for a Farrenfeugh person,' the Poppy explained gently.

'But I'm not a Farrenfeugh person: I heard the Pipe.'

'Part of you must be – I heard you singing one of our songs!' I thought about that for a moment. Then I said:

'But why does he hide them then?'

'To stop us from using them, of course. What questions you ask. He doesn't know that they always answer if they are called.'

'Oh! I see,' I said.

I didn't, really: there were lots of things I didn't see at all. But the Poppy's voice boomed indistinctly, as if I were sitting in a large bell, and it was difficult to hear what he was saying. So I sat there, snug and warm, peeping out from time to time, wondering where we were. Far beneath us I could see hills and woods, mountains and sometimes the distant sea. Now and then I thought I saw a group of fields, or a house or a cottage that I recognized, but I was never quite sure.

After what seemed a long long time, the Poppy began to float downwards. I poked my head out and saw that we had arrived at the edge of a huge frozen lake, surrounded by dark trees. Behind them vast mountains reared against the sky, black and forbidding; a thin covering of snow lay on the ground. It was very cold, and completely still and quiet: the sort of quiet that one expects to be broken at any moment.

'Come, we must hurry,' the Poppy whispered. 'I can smell thunder in the air! Have you got the Pipe?' Shivering with cold and excitement, I took the Pipe from my pocket, and the Poppy's voice rang out suddenly in the frozen silence.

'Pipe! Pipe! Show us the way.' The tinkling music I had heard before sounded again, and to my surprise the little Pipe wrenched from my hands, and began to jump, end on, in leaps and bounds across the lake.

'This is where Farrenfeugh ends and the Giant's domain begins,' the Poppy said, as we followed, slipping and stumbling on the ice. 'The Pipe will show us the way through.'

I found it hard to believe, but it was true. The Pipe had already stopped at the end of a large hole in the ice, and in a moment we had joined it. I looked down expecting to see water, But inside, it was round like a well. Cut out of the solid ice, steps led down into the depths. We stood at the edge, peering down into the darkness below.

'You must go on alone now,' the Poppy said. 'I can go no further.'

'Down there?' I said. I didn't like the idea at all. 'Down there alone?'

The Poppy twisted and turned on its stalk, bending his great head towards me.

'What shall we do?' he said finally. 'I can't go with you;

my magic goes no farther than this. Can't you go on alone? You will have the Silver Pipe to protect you!'

That's all very well, I thought, but the Pipe is very small, and that Giant, what I have seen of him, is very big! Then I remembered the poor unhappy Queen Bodina. And the King! What had happened to him?

'All right,' I said. 'I'll go – if you promise to wait for me here!'

'Of course I will wait,' the Poppy replied. 'When you reach the bottom, follow the Trembling River. There is always a boat waiting; tell it to take you to the King. You must find the King. If you need to, blow into the Pipe, it will know what to do. I will wait for you at the edge of the lake – by the trees. Good-bye, dear child. Good luck.'

I started down the steps. Light seemed to filter through from the surface of the lake, and it was not as dark as I had expected. But how cold it was: and it grew colder and colder, the farther I went. I thought the steps would go on for ever. Then, when I was beginning to feel giddy from going round and round, and round and round, they came to an end, and I found myself in a narrow winding tunnel. The only light there was seemed to come from white tree roots, which twisted their way in and out of the crumbling walls. Occasionally I heard scampering feet in some of the smaller passages and tunnels that I passed. I hurried along, stopping every now and then to peer round a corner, or into the mouth of another tunnel.

At last, when I was beginning to think I had lost my way, I saw in front of me a huge door, made entirely of tree-roots. There was a notice on it, in some strange language I could make neither head nor tail of. I was staring at it, trying to

find some recognizable word, when the door slowly opened and I found myself face to face with two giant rats, crouched side by side, entirely filling the doorway. They were several times my height, horrible-looking creatures – little wicked eyes, and sharp teeth yellowed and broken. They weren't going to let me pass, I could see, and they might well not stop at that. I took out the little Silver Pipe, and blew into it. To my delight, after only a second or two of silvery tinkling notes – which the Pipe played, not me, I've never played a note in my life – the rats closed their eyes, and went straight into a deep sleep. Shuddering slightly, I squeezed between them.

I was in an enormous rocky cavern, with arching sides, and a roof so far above my head, it was lost in darkness. Down the middle flowed a vast river. This must be the Trembling River, I thought. Indeed I knew it was. I could hear the water murmuring, 'tremble, tremble, tremble', as it swirled away into the gloom. Just in front of me, moored to the side, was a small boat. I jumped in, and said, in as commanding a voice as I could manage – 'Take me to the King! Please! As fast as you can.'

The boat must have been used to such orders, because there was no need to push off, it moved by itself, and we were soon out in mid-stream. All I could hear were drops of water plopping on to the seat beside me, and the swirling, swishing river murmuring tremble, tremble, tremble. The boat bumped and swayed; rocks loomed up in the darkness, but miraculously we always avoided them. Somewhere ahead, I heard a bell tolling. The tolling grew louder and gradually, as we came out into the open, I saw a large buoy with a bell in a cage on the top, rolling to and fro on the water. Beyond lay a desolate expanse of water, half-frozen, grey and still. Here and there, trees clustered together on tiny islands, poking their branches above the drifting mist.

The boat floated on, across the still surface of the lake, although there was no current that I could see, and finally we came to rest against a landing stage which jutted out from one of the larger islands. I hope nobody sees me, I thought, as I tied the boat to a post, and walked up on to the island amongst the trees.

The mist was thick and terribly cold. It was dark beneath the trees. I had no idea which way to go. So I took the Silver Pipe out of my pocket and blew into it. For a moment everything was just as before. But as I stood waiting for something to happen, I felt a draught blowing on the back of my neck, and a wind rushed past me, clearing a path through the mist. Following the wind, I ran up the path and there, behind an iron gate, its lower ramparts half-hidden by trees and mist, its battlements and turrets lost in the clouds above, stood a colossal castle. I was so small compared to it that I slipped through the gate easily, and at last stood gazing up at the towering mass. The walls were steep and slippery, but fortunately covered with a thick clinging creeper. I'll climb up that, I thought. Perhaps I'll find a window where I can get in.

The first window was shut tight; but the second was open. I pulled myself up on to the ledge and dropped down into the room inside. Looking round I saw I was in a sort of scullery, or pantry. It was vast! Everything in the room was ten sizes too big. The bucket under the sink was as big as a wardrobe.

Opposite me was a half-open door, through which I could smell food cooking. I crept to the door and peeped round the edge. In a kitchen the size of our barn at home stood a man with a tall white hat on his head, stirring something at a blackened stove. He was a giant, too, though not as big as the other one. Asleep beneath the table lay a black rat, as big as a dog, his eyes closed, and his long tail curled round the table legs. The fat Cook looked cross, and was talking to himself. '. . . two pinches of this . . . two pinches of that, it's enough to drive you crazy. And when I've cooked it I can hardly pick it up.' He slammed an iron tray on to the table, and then put on to it what looked like a dolls' tea service – a dolls' tea service to him, that is. Just the right size for me.

I know who that's for, I thought.

The fat Giant picked up the tray, still muttering and complaining, and waddled past me, the keys tied on to his belt gleaming and chinking in the firelight. I walked softly after him, keeping in the shadows as much as possible; across courtyards, through vast rooms, up and downstairs we went, until at last he stopped, unlocked a door, and went in, locking the door after him.

What shall I do now? I wondered. I couldn't even look through the keyhole. I took the Pipe out of my pocket, and blew into it. Immediately the most beautiful music imaginable began, quite different from before; almost like a full orchestra. Irresistible, I thought, and so it proved to be. In a

few moments the door was unlocked and the fat Giant popped his huge head out.

'Where's it coming from?' he said, looking up and down the passage.

'Don't tell me it's that tiny little creature making that beautiful sound,' he said finally, catching sight of me. 'Come in here, and play some more.'

'Lock the door again,' I said, when I was safely inside. Then I began to play again. He listened carefully for a moment or two, then slowly his eyes shut, and he too went straight off to sleep, leaning against the door jamb.

Now for the King, I thought, and ran into the centre of the room.

'Where are you, Your Majesty?' I shouted. My voice sounded like a tiny squeak in that great room. I called out again, and then listened. Was I wrong? Perhaps the King wasn't here at all. Perhaps I was in the wrong castle? Then faintly, from what seemed a long way off, I heard some banging, and an answering call.

Over in the corner stood a large wall cupboard with massive carved doors. The call had come from there. I stared up at the shiny, knobbly face of the cupboard. Could I get up there? It didn't look impossible. In fact it was easy; and soon I was struggling with the heavy brass catch which held the two doors together. I pushed and pulled, and tugged and strained; and finally one of the doors swung open, with a grinding creak. There, standing on a pile of linen, holding his silver crown in one hand, his beard and hair rough and untidy, stood the King. His magnificent robes were torn and dirty, but there was no mistaking him. He looked every inch a King. He seemed surprised to see a small, rather grubby little girl opening his prison door.

'Who are you?' he said, smiling.

'Your Majesty!' I whispered. I couldn't curtsey, as I was having quite a job hanging on to the brass catch. 'I'm – a – a – friend: I've not time to explain – we must get away from here, as quickly as we can.' No sooner had I said this than he had tucked up his long robes and was shinning down the side of the cupboard, as if he did it every day. We ran to the window.

'I can hear thunder,' the King said, gazing out across the lake.

'Quick then!' I put one leg out on to the sill. 'We can climb down here. It's lucky this creeper grows as far as it does.'

The climb down was more difficult than the climb up. It seemed much farther, and the height was dizzying. We were about half-way when something made me turn my head and look towards the lake. What I saw nearly made me fall. Striding across that huge expanse of water, for all the world like a child wading in a village pond, came Giant Slintingriel. Dangling from his belt were daggers and knives, and a long sword, studded with huge rubies, and over his shoulder was the red and blue cloak I had caught a glimpse of in the lane. Giants are red, giants are blue, I thought. I held my breath. What a terrifying spectacle he was! He looked as if he could pick up mountains with the greatest of ease, and smash them into powder. One great shaggy head, with its bulging eyes, stared before him, the other constantly peered behind. So wherever he was, he could see all round him. But fortunately he didn't catch sight of us hiding in the creeper.

As soon as he had vanished round the far side of the castle, we were down, and running towards the boat as if our lives depended on it; which of course they did. If only the boat were still there! What should we do if it had gone? But when we arrived at the landing stage, there it was nestling against the bank, like a dog that has been put on trust.

'Boat! Boat!' I cried, as we jumped in. 'Hurry; take us please – er – to where I found you!' Would that do? I couldn't think of the name. But the boat obviously understood where I meant, because it set off at what seemed a snail's pace across the lake. The mist had cleared, and we were in full view of Slintingriel's gigantic castle. I just prayed that, for the moment, no one would look out of the windows.

We had reached the buoy with its tolling bell before there were any signs of pursuit; and then far away, in between the tolling, we heard shouts, and sounds of commotion from the castle; and just as the boat nosed into the

entrance of the cavern, the King pointed behind us.
'Look,' he shouted. 'He's after us!'

It was true. We were into the gloom of the cavern by
now, and from this distance he looked small enough; but
far away as he was, I could make out the figure of Giant
Slintingriel striding after us. He still had some way to go;
it is difficult, even for a giant, to wade through deep and
partly frozen water in a hurry. But he was fast gaining on
us. I understood now why the river murmured tremble,
tremble, tremble, faintly in the darkness. I was trembling
too. The boat put on a sudden spurt of speed, as if it understood our plight. But behind us, as the tolling of the bell
grew fainter, we could hear the splashing of footsteps.

We had reached the bank and were racing from the boat
to the door, when he finally caught up with us, and planting
one huge wet foot firmly in front of the doorway, blocked
it, so that it was impossible to pass.

'HA! HA! HA!' he laughed, bending those two terrible
great heads down to have a closer look at us – at me, whom
he had not seen before. 'What have we here?'

All was lost, or so it seemed! We shrank against the wall,
paralysed with fright. Four great eyes glared out of the
darkness, and I could see, inches away, his huge dirty,
stubby fingers stretched towards us. He was almost there!
But at the last moment I recovered my wits, and snatching
the Silver Pipe from my pocket, blew into it as hard as I
could. Surprised by this unfamiliar sound, the Giant

hesitated; and immediately the two rats – whom I had forgotten all about, and who were still sprawled in the shadows on either side of the doorway – sprang to life. Leaping forward, they sank their sharp teeth into the Giant's foot as far as they would go.

There was a thunderous bellow from above, which almost split our ears. The Giant straightened up and started to hop about in the water, holding his injured foot, with the rats still clinging to it. We didn't wait to see any more: we were through that door in a moment, and running up the passage as fast as our legs would carry us. We never stopped once, not for a single instant, until we reached the open air; and there we sank, exhausted, on to the frozen surface of the lake.

The Poppy was waiting as he had promised he would, and after resting for a little while, we started on the long journey back to Farrenfeugh.

And now my memory fades a little, although certain things stand out clearly. The flat roof of the tower, crowded with people anxiously waiting for our return. The great cheer that rang out as they saw us approaching. The Queen's face, as the King held her in his arms again. But most of all, I remember the feast set out on long tables in the palace below, to celebrate our return and the defeat of Giant Slintingriel.

I sat on a small wooden chair, between the King and

Queen on their golden thrones. The Poppy hovered behind us; and all round us sat the strange Farrenfeugh people: the two tall stick soldiers, the Grasshopper Man, the round grey leather people, and the jewelled courtiers and palace officials. On the far side of the room, I noticed three more Poppies, in a group together – So they haven't all gone, I thought – and what food! I've never seen such an array of extraordinary dishes, although now I think of it, a strange thing, it was all in varying shades of green. Green soup; green meat sand vegetables; very pale green ice-cream, and a delicious assortment of fruit pies and tarts, all green too. Even the wine was green. I tried everything! Each dish was better than the last; when we could eat no more, we pulled crackers, and then sat round the fire eating chestnuts and reading the jokes from the crackers.

I suppose I might have stayed there for days, if I hadn't remembered my father's birthday.

'I think I ought to go now,' I said, getting to my feet rather suddenly. 'Oh!' they all cried. 'Not yet. Not yet, surely?' and the Queen leaned forward and offered me more ice-cream. But when I explained that my parents would worry, and anyway my father's birthday was coming the next day, the King shook my hand, and the Queen kissed me; and all the courtiers and soldiers clapped and shouted, and threw their hats in the air. Then they all crowded up the stairs, as we made our way to the top of the tower. 'We'll never forget you,' they shouted. 'Good-bye!

Good-bye! Come back and see us one day.' I watched them waving their handkerchiefs, getting smaller and smaller, their voices fainter and fainter, as the Poppy and I floated higher and ever higher. At last I could hear and see them no more.

The Poppy took me back to the lane where we first met, and after having said good-bye several times, soared away into the sky, and disappeared into the shimmering blue far above. I collected my bait-pot, and walked home slowly, thinking about my adventures. When I got home, it was tea-time, and my mother couldn't understand why I wasn't at all hungry.

Since then, I sometimes think of the strange Farrenfeugh people, and hope that they are safe and well. And every time I pick a red poppy in the summer-time, I hope it will be the one from Farrenfeugh. Until now it never has been. But, of course, you might be lucky one day.

If you have enjoyed reading this book and would like to know about others which we publish, why not join the Puffin Club? You will be sent the club magazine, *Puffin Post*, four times a year and a smart badge and membership book. You will also be able to enter all the competitions. For details of cost and an application form, send a stamped addressed envelope to:

The Puffin Club Dept A
Penguin Books Limited
Bath Road, Harmondsworth
Middlesex